MW00902818

Toby's Big Truck Adventure

Reta Spears-Stewart

Toby's Big Truck Adventure

Reta Spears-Stewart

Pacific Press Publishing Association
Boise, Idaho
Oshawa, Ontario, Canada

Edited by Jerry D. Thomas
Designed by Dennis Ferree
Cover Art by Mark Stutzman
Inside Art by Georgina Larson
Typeset in 13/16 Century Schoolbook

Copyright © 1993 by
Pacific Press Publishing Association
Printed in United States of America
All Rights Reserved

Library of Congress Cataloging-in-Publication Data:
Spears-Stewart, Reta.
  Toby's big truck adventure / by Reta Spears-Stewart.
    p.   cm.
  Summary: After finishing the second grade Toby, in search of
friends and interesting pets, goes trucking with Uncle Dan and
finds that following God is the biggest adventure of all.
  ISBN 0-8163-1141-2
  [1. Christian life—Fiction. 2. Trucks—Fiction. 3. Uncles—
Fiction.] I. Title.
PZ7.S74115To   1993   92-35750
  [Fic] — dc20   CIP
                                                  AC

93 94 95 96 97 ● 5 4 3 2 1

Dedication

**For the real truckers:
my son Dan and his nephew, George.**

Contents

Chapter 1 A Rat for a Friend 9

Chapter 2 Ratoid! 17

Chapter 3 Good News for Supper 24

Chapter 4 Big Truck Adventure 29

Chapter 5 Beans, Cornbread, and Rules. . . 35

Chapter 6 A Truckin' Dog 41

Chapter 7 Cookie Breath 46

Chapter 8 Goodbye to Berf. 51

Chapter 9 Sharing a Loaf by the Sea 56

Chapter 10 Surprise, Surprise, Surprise! . . . 67

Chapter 11 A Treehouse Disaster 73

Chapter 12 A Dead Bird and a Road Sign . . 81

Chapter 13 The Biggest Adventure of All . . . 89

Chapter 1

A Rat
for a Friend

I hate moving. Especially at the beginning of summer vacation. And at the end of second grade.

When you're a new kid in town, summer gets boring. That's why I'm glad that Uncle Dan is coming with his big truck. Mom told me just this morning.

She said, "Toby, Uncle Dan is coming to see us this summer. He has invited you to ride along with him in his truck for a few days. Maybe a week."

I held my breath. Uncle Dan is the best. Sometimes when he had a trucking trip near our old house, he would stop in to see us. I didn't know if he ever had trucking trips near where we live now. But now he's coming to visit his sister—my mom—and me.

He always bunches up my hair and says, "Hey, Toby, how's my good buddy?" Then we pretend to punch each other and goof around.

"Would you like to go trucking with Uncle Dan, Toby?" Mom asked (as if she really needed to!).

"YES!" I shouted, letting myself breathe again. "*Yes!*" I said again. This would be my first trip in the truck for more than one day. "But when is he coming?"

"He's not sure yet. But sometime soon," she answered.

So for now, I had no friends and nothing to do. Then I had a great idea. What I needed was a pet! And I knew just the right kind.

"Not a big pet," I told Mom. "Just something small I could talk to and play with."

"And take care of?" asked Mom.

"Well, sure," I agreed.

"What did you have in mind, Toby?"

"I was thinking about a rat," I said.

She looked like I said I was thinking of shaving my eyebrows.

"A rat!" she said. Then she stared at me for a few seconds. "But why?" she asked.

"Rats are not bad," I said. "At least not the cool ones they have at Ned's Pet Store."

"Cool?"

"Sure. They're different colors. They're clean. They're soft and furry. And Ned said they eat practically anything."

Mom opened her mouth to say something else, but nothing came out. I kept talking.

"Rats are smart. And they only cost two dollars this week." It was time for the clincher. "And there is a little black-and-white one that really needs a home." I thought that would win her over.

"Besides, Mom," I reminded her, "one of your rules is that people should not make up their minds before they have all the facts."

"Rats," she said.

"One rat," I said.

"Well, I guess a rat wouldn't bark, anyway," said Mom.

"Let's see, this is Tuesday. OK, we'll go have a look at Ned's Pet Store on Thursday. I'll be finished sewing Mrs. Matthews' new suit by then."

Mom's job is making clothes and stuff for other women. She says it's a good job for her to have. That way, she can be at home when I am. She's good at it, I guess, because I hear the sewing machine *whirrr-r-ring* in her sewing room a lot. And she can hear what's happening in the rest of the house—usually.

On Wednesday, she missed it.

I was supposed to be washing the lunch dishes. That's another of Mom's rules—we wash dishes right after we eat. But I was thinking of the fort I wanted to build for my lizard, Bob. He's made of rubber, but he's an OK toy sometimes. Besides, I thought, a rat might need a fort too.

I left the dishes and found a couple of shoe boxes in my room. I taped them together in a T shape. I cut a little door between them. Next, I added an empty milk carton for a tower.

By then, the fort looked pretty cool. It even had a little flag I made from one of Mom's sewing scraps. All the fort needed was a four-wheeler for Bob (or a rat) to go scouting in. I cut a big hole in the side of an empty salt box. It was perfect. But what about the wheels?

Then I had a great idea. Bobbins! Those little round metal spools Mom used for thread in her sewing machine. I knew she had a box of bobbins without any thread in them. And I had seen her put them up on her closet shelf.

The bobbins were flat, round, silver, and had holes in the center. In fact, they *looked* like little wheels. Four bobbins would be perfect.

I could still hear *whirrr-r-ring* from the sewing room. I won't bother Mom, I thought. I pushed a chair from the kitchen into Mom's bedroom. I felt a little guilty going in her room when she wasn't there. I felt more guilty climbing on the chair to reach the closet shelf. And I was feeling a *lot* guilty about taking down her box of bobbins.

Suddenly, the chair slipped out from under me. I went flying. Bobbins were everywhere. Mom heard the crash. I was still tangled in the upside-down chair when she got there.

First she asked, "Are you OK, Toby?"

I said, "Uh-huh."

Then she got mad. "Toby Dean, why were you in my closet?"

"Uh, I needed four bobbins," I answered.

"Four of *my* bobbins?" she asked.

"Uh-huh," I mumbled.

"From *my* closet?"

"Yes," I said very quietly.

She sat on her bed and looked out the window.

I pulled the chair out of her closet. Then I began picking up bobbins.

"Toby?" said Mom.

"Yes, Mom?"

"How did you feel when you took my bobbins without asking me?"

"I didn't want to interrupt your work, Mom," I said.

"But you interrupted your own work, Toby."

"The dishes," I said.

Mom nodded and looked out the window again.

Then she said, "Toby, I think we need to talk about respect here. For other people, sure. But for yourself too."

"What do you mean?" I asked. But I think I really knew the answer.

"If you have a bad feeling about doing something, it's probably your conscience," Mom said. "God gave us a conscience for a very good reason. Sometimes you will feel guilty inside about doing something. Like you would not like anyone to see you do it.

"That's when you should ask yourself, 'Would this make the Lord proud of me?' If the answer is 'I don't think so,' you had better not do it."

"Then will I respect myself?"

"It will be a good start." Mom smiled.

I handed her the box of bobbins. Then I started to push the chair back into the kitchen.

"Toby," said Mom, "I want you to finish the dishes. Then we will talk about rats . . . and other friends."

I was putting the last clean dish away when Mom came into the kitchen.

"I think we need a cookie break," said Mom. I agreed pretty quickly.

"I'll pour the milk while you get the Oreo cookies," Mom said. "They are on the bottom shelf in the pantry."

I found the cookies and was already munching my second one by the time she had our glasses filled.

Mom said, "Toby, I don't know why you would want a rat."

I started to answer, but she wasn't finished.

"But I know you need a friend. And I'm sure pet rats are not at all like the wild ones. So we will look into it on Thursday, as I promised."

I said a quiet "Yippee." And took a third cookie.

Mom said, "I think you need to make some human friends too."

"I had human friends in our old town," I said. "Lots of them. But this town is boring. Everybody has gone somewhere else for the summer. There are no other kids around. And school doesn't start for two whole months."

I helped myself to a fourth cookie. Mom closed the package and put it away. "I saw a boy about your age yesterday," she said. "I think he lives in the house behind ours." She had one of her "thinking" looks. "Let's see now," she added. "Doesn't the Bible say something about how to make friends?"

I grinned and said, " 'Show ourselves friendly.' "

"That might be worth a try." Mom smiled.

"Mm-hmm," I said, wiping my milk mustache off with my sleeve.

"Toby!" Mom said.

"Oops." That broke another rule. "Sorry," I said, and headed for the door.

Chapter 2

Ratoid!

On Thursday morning, there was a knock on the front door. It was the kid who lives in the house in back of ours.

"I'm Kevin," he said. "You're new, aren't you?"

Kevin was carrying a large, rolled-up paper. He was dressed in a green T-shirt. It was splattered with paint or something. His purple pants were dirty. His shoes didn't match—they were two kinds of tennis shoes. He wore orange socks. And I think he had not combed his hair for most of his life.

I decided he was trouble.

"My name is Toby," I said. But not too friendly. "We moved here last week."

"Where ya from?" Kevin asked.

"Chicago," I answered. Then I asked, "Where do you go to school?"

"Chicago! Yuck," he said, instead of answering my question.

I gave him another chance. "I'll be going to

Roberts Elementary. Where do you go?"

"Roberts," Kevin said.

Oh, no-o-o, I thought.

"Ya want to play or something?" Kevin asked.

He just walked past me into the living room.

"Like what?" I asked. But I was not too excited about it. This kid was really grungy looking.

"I know a cool game," he answered. "Got any cookies?"

"Cookies?" I repeated.

"Yeah. We need twelve cookies for the game," Kevin said. "You get the cookies. I'll set up the game," he ordered.

Then he began to unroll the large paper. It had squares and circles drawn on it. Like a map of some kind. I went to the kitchen for the Oreo cookies. I heard the sewing machine *whirrr-r-ring*. I heard Kevin's paper rattling. I took the package of Oreo cookies off the shelf.

In the living room, I handed the package to Kevin. He opened it and began to lay cookies on some of the game circles and squares.

Then he said, "We also need a piece of red cloth. Does your mom have one?"

This is dumb, I thought. But I went to Mom's sewing-scrap bag in the kitchen. After pulling out about twenty scraps of cloth, I found a red one.

"Here is the red cloth," I called on my way back to the living room.

Kevin was gone.

And so was the package of Oreo cookies—except for six that still lay on the big paper.

So, it was all a trick, I thought. "Ooooh!" I yelled. "That jerk! That rotten kid!"

It wasn't just the stolen cookies. It was being tricked that made me so mad. I kicked the paper "game" still spread on the floor. Paper and cookies flew all over. The sewing machine in the other room became awfully quiet.

"I hate him!" I yelled again. I guess I really wanted Mom to come and see what was going on.

She did. "What's the fuss about?"

"This grungy kid came over and stole our Oreos!" I shouted.

"Calm down and tell me about it," Mom said. I told her the whole thing. Maybe I even made the story a little more exciting. Like pointing out that the boy was slightly bigger than I. And that he was probably part of a gang.

I knew Mom was trying not to smile at that last part.

"Well, he could have been," I said. I smiled a little myself.

"That does seem like a dirty trick," said Mom. "But maybe there is a reason for what Kevin did."

Then she looked around and said, "Why don't you pick up the paper and broken cookies?" It was not really a question. "I'll talk to Kevin's mother."

"Fine!" I said. But I was still mad.

Then I noticed the look in Mom's eye and quickly added, "I mean, that's fine. I'll pick up the cookies." Mom went back to her sewing room. And I cleaned up the mess I had made. Then I worked on painting my model dinosaur until lunch.

But I still got mad when I thought of Kevin. I should have known, I thought. A kid dressed like that couldn't be anything but bad news.

I tried to make myself think of good stuff. Like getting a pet rat that afternoon.

And teaching it to chase Kevin.

After lunch, Mom said, "OK, let's go to Ned's Pet Store."

I jumped up and yelled, "All right!"

"But we are just going to get the facts," said Mom. "I have not promised to buy you a rat."

"I know," I said. But I still had a secret hope. On the way to Ned's, we talked about pets. I asked Mom what pet she liked most when she was a kid.

"I had a little rabbit once," Mom said. Then she laughed. "It happened to be a black-and-white one. And I begged my parents for two weeks before they said Yes." She looked at me for a second. "I had to promise to take care of it all by myself."

"I'd do that!" I said.

"It's not as easy as it seems," Mom said. "You have to feed pets every day. They need fresh, clean water in their cage all the time."

"I knew that."

"And you have to clean out their cages. It's not fun when they go to the bathroom in their cages."

I made a face. But I said, "I can handle that."

"Of course, it could help you learn some things," Mom said.

"Oh, it would," I said helpfully.

"Well, we do have that old birdcage in the attic."

Then I almost messed up everything. I heard myself say quietly, "I'd like to stuff Kevin in it."

I didn't say it quietly enough, though.

"We need to talk about your attitude," Mom said. "Remember about getting all the facts before you make up your mind?"

"But, Mom, Kevin is grungy looking. And he stole our cookies."

"Toby, do you remember the story in the Bible about the raggedy-looking man in the book of James?"

"Yes," I said, "they made him sit all by himself. Just because of how he was dressed."

I thought about that for a minute.

Then I said, "But, Mom, he stole our cookies."

Mom turned the car down Main Street. I knew the pet store was not far. And I knew Mom was thinking about something besides rats.

"I saw Kevin's mother in their yard last night," she said. "I was glad to meet her. And to ask about

Kevin. Toby, they are very poor. Kevin has no father, either. And his mother has been very ill. She cannot work yet to get money for a lot of things. They have not had things like cookies for a long time."

I began to feel a little sorry for Kevin and his mom. "Well, he didn't have to trick me to get some stupid cookies, did he?"

"Maybe he didn't start out to trick you," Mom said.

"Huh?"

"Maybe seeing all those cookies was just too much for him." Then she asked, "Have you ever done something wrong? And then been sorry?"

Mom knew I had—just yesterday afternoon.

"It sure is good to be forgiven, isn't it?" she said. Then we were at Ned's Pet Store.

The black-and-white rat was still there. Mom talked to Ned for a while. I think she asked him forty thousand questions about rats. At last, she smiled and said, "OK, we'll take him. And we'll need some rat food too."

I almost yelled "Yayy-y-y!" right there in the store. But I waited until we got in the car. I yelled so loud I think I scared the soup out of the little rat.

He was in a cardboard carton on my lap. When I yelled, he started racing around and around. Then he looked up at me. I imagined him thinking, "Ho, boy—this will not be boring."

"What will you name your new friend?" Mom asked.

"Ratoid," I said. I had decided that days ago.

"Very interesting name," she said. "And one more important thing," Mom added. "Be sure to keep the cage door closed when you are not in the room."

Chapter 3

Good News
for Supper

Ratoid was lost. And it was my fault.

I had him only one week. And Mom had warned me—"Keep the cage door closed when you're not in the room."

But when I remembered my favorite TV program, I forgot everything else. One little "forget," and Ratoid was out of his cage. And out the open window.

I admit I cried when I discovered he was gone. And crying is not cool for a guy in going-on-third grade. But I really liked that little rat.

Mom could have been mad that I didn't take her warning. But she must have known how bad I felt. All she said about it was, "Sometimes what happens when you mess up is punishment enough. That's called 'suffering the consequences.'"

I sure was suffering the consequences, all right.

At supper that night, I didn't eat much. I just pushed my food around on my plate with my fork. Tator-Tot potatoes with melted cheese is one of my favorites. But I just wasn't hungry.

"Toby," Mom said, "you've really had a bad time lately, haven't you?"

"Yeah," I said. I tried to swallow. It felt like there was a basketball in my throat.

"I know you have been bored and lonesome since we moved," she said.

"Yeah," I agreed again. Then I changed the subject.

"I talked to Kevin this morning. He might be a friend, after all. He said he was sorry he tricked me. He told me there really is a game with cookies. And he will show me when they get some. Plus, he likes dinosaurs. And making stuff.

"But today he is leaving to visit his grandma in another town. He will be gone for two weeks."

Mom put her cup down. She reached over to push my hair off my forehead. "Well, I have good news for you, Toby. Your Uncle Dan called this afternoon. He's on his way here. He has a truck-load of pop bottles to deliver in Illinois, and he wants you to go trucking with him."

I just stared at her with my mouth hanging open.

"You still want to go, don't you?" she asked.

"Yes!" I finally shouted. I jumped up from the table. "Will he be here tonight?"

"No, no," she laughed. "Sit down. He'll be here in the morning."

I sat down slowly. This was almost too good to be true. Just Uncle Dan and me, I thought. Moms are great, but sometimes a guy needs to be with guys.

"I'll go pack my stuff," I said out loud.

"Hold on," Mom said with a smile. "Don't you think you'd better finish eating your supper?"

Suddenly I was hungry again. I crammed three Tator-Tot potatoes into my mouth at once.

"And your room has to be in A-1 order before you leave," Mom said.

"OK," I said. I ate the last of my chocolate pudding and wiped my upper lip with my sleeve.

"Toby, not again!" Mom scolded.

"Heh-heh. Sorry," I said. But I remembered to say, "May I be excused?"

"Go." Mom smiled.

I sailed up the stairs. But I heard Mom holler, "Brush your teeth!"

In my room I picked up five books off the floor.

And some stamps I was thinking of collecting.

And an apple core.

And about twelve cents.

And a pair of underwear.

I folded up the huge map I was drawing of my new neighborhood. I hung up my raincoat and church shirt. I even brushed my teeth.

Then I packed most of the stuff I thought I'd need for the trip. Later, Mom checked it out.

She added a sweater and an extra pair of clean socks.

She subtracted the football and the marble collection.

But she did leave the baseball cards and the tablet and colored pencils in my suitcase.

She stared at Bob, the rubber lizard, for a few seconds. Then she stuffed him back in my bag.

After packing, Mom and I said our prayers together.

"Dear God, thanks for letting me go trucking with Uncle Dan," I said. "I'm sorry I said I hate Kevin the other day—and left Ratoid's cage open."

"Protect Toby and Dan as they travel, Lord Jesus," Mom said, "and help Toby be the best he can be."

We said "Amen" and hugged, like always. But my eyes didn't want to close that night. I thought it would take forever for morning to come.

Chapter 4

Big Truck Adventure

The sound of hissing brakes on the big eighteen-wheeler woke me.

It was Friday morning. Uncle Dan was here. And I would be a trucker for maybe a whole week.

I jumped out of bed to see Uncle Dan.

He lifted me up and said, "Whoa, this fellow is as big as a horse!" Then he bunched up my hair and said, "Hey, good buddy. You ready to go trucking?"

Was I ever! I was glad to have some real adventure in my summer. I was glad to be off with another guy for a change. And I was glad to be away from rules for a while. I was just about sick of rules.

The thought of traveling in a truck across the country—with no rules—was exciting. I felt really old—maybe even twenty.

When you're trucking, Mom can't remind, "Bedtime at eight o'clock," or "Remember to brush your teeth."

Mom made some of her special trucker flap jacks for breakfast. They were super big and stacked high, filled with cherries. But I was so excited I could hardly eat mine.

At last, we headed across the yard to the truck. I tossed my suitcase up to Uncle Dan. He was sitting behind the steering wheel in the truck. I grabbed the metal handle above the back wheel of the truck cab. Then pulled myself up to a foothold.

I turned and gave Mom a quick hug. " 'Bye," I said in my most grown-up voice. She gave me a pat, and I scrambled into the truck.

Uncle Dan called to Mom over the noise of the engine. "Don't worry about us truckers now. The Lord is traveling with us."

"I know." Mom smiled. "Now, have a great time, you two. And obey all the rules."

"We'll call you tomorrow night," called Uncle Dan. Mom waved as the truck began to roll forward.

"Rules!" I muttered. But my grump fizzled in the hiss of the truck's air brakes. I felt the big engine rumble under me. My stomach felt funny, like there were eighty-nine butterflies inside. Truckers Toby and Dan were on their way.

We turned onto a ramp to the highway. Uncle Dan said, "Let's ask Jesus to help drive this truck, OK?"

"Sure," I answered. I folded my hands on my lap.

"Kind of a little rule of mine," added Uncle Dan. I folded my hands a little tighter.

Uncle Dan finished praying, and I said Amen. Then I asked, "What do you mean 'rule'?"

Uncle Dan looked at me for a quick second. Then he chuckled and said, "Oh, praying's not a real rule. It's just something important to me. I always remind myself to pray."

"I'm glad it's not a rule," I said, "because rules are really starting to bother me."

"Well, say now," Uncle Dan said. "Truckers do have rules—and good truckers try to obey them."

I decided not to say anything about that. Instead, I asked, "Uncle Dan, could I climb back and ride in the bunk behind you?"

"Sure," Uncle Dan said. "But take your shoes off so you don't get our bed dirty. That's the . . ."

"Rule," I finished his sentence. Then I climbed back into the high sleeping area behind the seats. The ride on the bed was a lot smoother. And I felt safe and snug there. I could also hear Uncle Dan better there.

From my high place, I watched factories glide by. We headed out of town. Farmhouses began to appear. And a lot of cows and horses on the rolling hills.

Uncle Dan knew the names of several kinds of cows. Pretty soon he said, "I'm hungry. How about you, Toby?"

"Me too."

"Let's break out the lunch your mom packed for us. There are some cold drinks there too."

We began munching egg-salad sandwiches and corn chips. Uncle Dan turned on the CB radio.

"We'll just see if anything important is happening," he said.

A voice from the radio crackled, "This is Red Fred. How 'bout a southbounder-eighteen?"

I knew that "Red Fred" was the radio name or "handle" of some trucker. But I wasn't sure about "southbounder-eighteen." Uncle Dan explained.

"That means the trucker is looking for someone driving south on Highway 18. If Red Fred is heading south, they can travel together."

Another voice came over the CB.

"This is Dinosaur, southbound-18. Heading into Mollie's for gas and dumplings. Bring 'er back."

I thought Dinosaur was a cool "handle." And I remembered "bring 'er back" was one CB way to say, "It's your turn to talk."

"This is Red Fred," the first voice said. "I'll meet you at Mollie's, Dinosaur. I'm out."

"Are we going to stop at Mollie's too?" I asked Uncle Dan.

"Well, Mollie's Truck Stop does have good food," answered Uncle Dan. "But we'll be past there when it's time to stop for supper."

Just then, another voice crackled over the CB.

"Breaker. I've got a ten-thirty-six. Mile marker two-zero-three."

"That's an accident," Uncle Dan whispered. He listened closely to the radio.

The voice continued. "Gonna be a big traffic jam. Think the trucker was going too fast down 'Dead Man's Curve.' "

I swallowed hard.

"Uncle Dan," I said in a whisper like his. "Do you think anyone was hurt?"

"I don't know, Toby. The accident is behind us. But we can pray, can't we?"

"Sure," I answered. I folded my hands again.

"Dear Jesus," I started, "if anyone was hurt in that accident, please help them." I peeked at Uncle Dan. "And help the drivers remember the speeding rules."

"I'll 'amen' that!" Uncle Dan said. "Now we better pull into this 'chicken coop.' "

"That's a weigh station, Uncle Dan. I remember that."

"You're right, pal. Trucks can only carry so much weight on certain roads. Otherwise the roads would wear out too soon. Some truckers call the weigh stations 'chicken coops.' That's because they are such little buildings. The scales here are special. They can weigh the whole truck at once," Uncle Dan said.

"The 'Weigh Master' is the boss at weigh stations. And all trucks must stop and be weighed," said Uncle Dan. "It's the rule."

"Wow," I said. We pulled onto the huge platform scales. The Weigh Master looked our truck over. He wrote some numbers on a clipboard. Then he smiled and waved us on. We were on our way again.

Uncle Dan turned the CB off. I watched out the window for a while. Then I got a little sleepy. I curled up with a pillow. Bob, the rubber lizard, stood guard.

I fell asleep thinking about Ratoid. Then Uncle Dan woke me up when he said, "Hungry, Toby?"

Chapter 5

Beans, Cornbread, and Rules

"You've had quite a snooze, Toby," Uncle Dan said. I rubbed my eyes and looked out the truck window. It was dark already. The farmhouses were just clumps of lights.

I yawned and stretched. I said, "My stomach has the growls. Are we going to eat at a truck stop?"

"We sure are," said Uncle Dan. "Better get yourself awake. Tom's Truck Stop is only about five minutes from here."

"Do they have a 'supper special'?" I asked. I tried to sound like a trucker.

"Best beans and cornbread and pie this side of the Mississippi," laughed Uncle Dan.

I stuffed Bob in my suitcase and rubbed my face awake. We were pulling into Tom's Truck Stop. Uncle Dan stopped the truck and got out. I pulled on my shoes and climbed out after him.

First, we took a shower at the truck stop. Then we ordered two trucker-size bowls of beans with cornbread. And warm apple pie with ice cream on top.

After that, Uncle Dan and I took a walk. We walked down a little road beside the truck stop. Every star was trying to shine brighter than the rest. They seemed close enough to touch.

We didn't talk much. But I was thinking a lot. Back at the truck I said, "I thought there weren't many rules for truckers."

I grabbed the handle on the side of the truck cab and climbed up. Uncle Dan was right behind me. He said, "There will always be rules, partner."

"But I hate rules!"

"Why?"

We climbed up into the wide bunk behind the seats. I said, "Rules mean somebody always telling you what to do. Then, they get mad when you mess up." I looked at Uncle Dan. "I doubt if anybody would do that to a trucker!"

We pulled off our shoes and crawled under the big, soft blanket. "Hey, pal, you've got it wrong. Truckers have lots of rules."

"They do?" I was a little surprised. But not too much, now that I knew the rules about speeding. And truck weights.

"Well, sure," Uncle Dan went on. "Truckers have rules about their rigs. They have to check everything for safety every day. The tires, the brakes, the 'fifth wheel' that holds the tractor and trailer together. Even the windshield wipers have to be checked. That's the rule."

"OK, but . . ." I started to say.

Uncle Dan went on. "Truckers have to keep 'logs.' That means write down how many hours and miles they drive each day. It's the rule. If they drive over the limit, they can get too tired," Uncle Dan said. "They could even fall asleep while they are driving."

"Wow!" I said. "I never thought of that. They could have a wreck if that happened."

"It sometimes happens," said Uncle Dan. "And there are rules about the CB radio. We have to talk over certain channels. And wait and take turns when we talk."

"I didn't know there were all those rules."

"There are a lot more rules too," said Uncle Dan. "And they all have a reason. But this is the important thing. Because we are friends of Jesus, you and I should always obey the rules."

"Oh, yes," I agreed.

"Do you know why?" asked Uncle Dan.

I didn't think about it long. "Because Jesus is also our Boss? And He said so?"

"Well, yes," laughed Uncle Dan. "But there is more to it. Jesus loves us and wants to take care of us. So, He put certain people in charge of us. When we obey our parents, we are letting Jesus take care of us. It's the same with teachers, police officers, or Weigh Masters."

That made a whole lot of sense even to me.

I said, "That's different."

Uncle Dan laughed. He plopped a pillow on my head. "So stop talking," he chuckled. "Let's say our prayers and go to sleep. We've got a big day ahead of us tomorrow."

"OK, partner," I said, grinning in the dark. I prayed for another chance to have a pet. But I would have never guessed how fast my prayer would be answered.

Chapter 6

A Truckin' Dog

I think as soon as I said Amen I fell asleep. I mean fast. And morning came with a bang. Or maybe I should say with a bark.

I woke up because I thought I heard barking outside the truck. At first I thought I was dreaming, but then, there it was again. It sounded more like a squeak than a real bark.

"Uncle Dan," I said. "Wake up. There's a dog or something outside the truck." It was barely light out.

"A dog?" Uncle Dan yawned. He looked at his watch. "Six-thirty. I guess we better get rolling." Then we both heard the squeaky bark.

Uncle Dan sat up so fast he bumped his head. "Oof!" he said. "Woof!" we heard outside the truck. Only it was more like "werf."

We both scrambled to the window and looked out. One very small, yellow dog sat by our door. His ears were long and floppy. He was looking up at us.

"Well, I'll be," said Uncle Dan. "I wonder where he's from."

We pulled our shoes on and slid out of the bunk. The little dog watched as we climbed out of the truck. He tipped his head to one side and barked again. It was a quiet little bark. It sounded a lot like he was asking, "Werf?"

"Cute little fellow," said Uncle Dan. "He probably belongs to the truck stop. Let's go find some breakfast, pal."

I was starving, so it sounded great to me. I followed Uncle Dan toward the truck-stop restaurant. And the little dog followed me.

At the door, Uncle Dan stopped. He petted the dog on the head. "I don't think you are supposed to go in here, fellow," he said.

"Werf," said the dog.

Inside, Uncle Dan said to the man behind the cash register, "You've got two hungry men here." Then he nodded his head toward the door and asked, "That your dog?"

"Naw," said the man. "He's nobody's dog, I guess."

"What makes you say that?" asked Uncle Dan.

"A couple of days ago an eighteen-wheeler pulled in here for fuel," answered the man. "Before they pulled out, they opened the cab door. The little yellow pup just rolled out. Guess they just didn't want to feed him anymore."

"Wow," I said. "That's mean."

"Happens every now and then," said the man. "Guess they figure someone will take care of them. But this little guy has almost been run over a couple of times already. He doesn't seem to know what to do."

All during breakfast I kept asking Uncle Dan questions.

"What if *nobody* wants the puppy? What if he gets run over? What if he starves to death? What if a bigger dog fights him? Or a wildcat eats him? What if . . ."

"Maybe he needs a boy to watch out for him," said Uncle Dan. He didn't look up.

"Yeah!" I agreed. "That's what he needs, all right."

"I guess I'll have to leave you here. Then you can take care of the little dog," Uncle Dan agreed.

He almost fooled me that time. Uncle Dan is always kidding me. "Huh-uh," I laughed. "I think he needs a ride in a truck," I said, kidding back.

Uncle Dan put down his empty cup and wiped his mouth with his napkin.

"A dog is a Major League commitment," he said. "It involves everybody in the family."

"I know," I said, with that old lump in my throat. "Mom probably would say No. Besides, a dog barks. She says that makes her sewing customers nervous."

I added, "Of course, this little dog squeaks more than barks."

"A dog can be taught not to bark," Uncle Dan said. I almost let myself hope again.

"And this dog doesn't cost anything," I said. "He would probably eat a lot of leftover stuff."

Uncle Dan laughed. "You might make a good salesman someday." He left some tip money on the table for the waitress, just to thank her for doing a good job. Then we walked toward the register man.

"Actually, I've been thinking of getting a dog myself," Uncle Dan said. "A dog would be good company to have with me on these trips. I suppose we could take him along. If your Mom says OK, he will be your dog. If not, he'll be my trucking dog. How does that sound?"

I said, very quietly, "It sounds just fine."

But I wanted to yell "Yahooooo!" Which I did—when we got outside. The little dog seemed to know we were his new friends. But then, he had come to our truck, after all. Almost like he had picked us out.

He scrambled right up into the truck. Uncle Dan gave him a little help. He seemed to belong there. He jumped right back into the bunk and lay down in a little ball. His head rested on his front paw. He looked at us with bright, happy eyes.

Uncle Dan said, "Well, I guess he's saying Thanks. Maybe we should do the same thing."

I didn't need to hear it twice. I folded my hands and started to pray.

"Dear God, thank You for letting the puppy come to our truck. Maybe You want me to keep him," I said, peeking at Uncle Dan. "If You do, help Uncle Dan talk Mom into it. Amen."

"Amen," said Uncle Dan. Then he said, "Me?"

"Well, she'll probably listen more to her brother," I said.

"I'm not the one who will be taking care of him at your house."

"I'll practice while we finish the trip," I said.

"I won't be the one who will buy his food."

"I'll rake neighbors' leaves and stuff to earn money for dog food."

"I won't be the one who cleans up after him."

"I know how to do it."

"I won't be the one to see that he always has fresh water—and that the gate is always closed."

Ouch, I thought. But I knew what he meant.

"I think I learned my lesson," I said. "I suffered the consequences. Besides," I added with a grin, "it was your idea."

"Werf," laughed the little yellow dog. And I laughed again too.

Chapter 7

Cookie Breath

I asked the little yellow dog, "What's your name, boy?"

"Berf!" he answered. So that's what we called him.

Berf was used to riding in a truck. You could tell. He would sit for a while on the bunk. He watched cars and trucks go by. His floppy ears would move toward any sound. When the air brakes hissed, he sat very still.

When the CB crackled, he stretched toward it and said, "Werf?"

When Uncle Dan and I talked, he curled up and pretended to nap. I think he got bored when we talked.

But when we stopped for gas or food, Berf was the first one by the door. He squeezed between me and Uncle Dan. Then he looked out the window and said, "Roof!"

Outside, Uncle Dan would check things on the truck. Berf and I would run around on any grass near the truck. He would drink water I put in a pan for him. Then he would smell a lot of trees and bushes.

Finally, Uncle Dan would call, "Let's go!" And Berf and I would jump back in the truck.

Inside, Berf and I would play games. One game was with a rolled-up sock. I let him smell the sock really well. Then I hid it somewhere in the bunk.

"Sniff," he would say. "Snerf, snoof, snort."

He would sniff under the blanket. He would snort under the pillows. He would slide his wet nose under my shirt and go, "Snoof?" I would laugh until I fell over.

Then he would find the sock. And wiggle his back end like crazy. "Funff!" Berf would say with a mouth full of sock. I knew he was really saying, "I won!"

When we stopped to eat, Berf stayed in the truck. We brought him a giant hamburger for his supper.

"No pickles or onions," Uncle Dan said. After we let him run around a little, we all climbed back in the truck. When it got almost dark, we pulled into a rest stop that Uncle Dan knew. It was clean and had trees and picnic tables. We used the restrooms and settled down in the bunk. Berf slept on the front seat. I thought, This is great. I wish we could just keep on trucking.

But on the second day we had Berf, things changed. Uncle Dan switched on the CB. It crackled, and we heard a different voice. It was a kid.

"This is Cookie Breath. Anyone seen my dog?" I took a quick breath. Berf tipped his head to one side and looked at the radio. Both of his ears went forward.

Another voice crackled through the CB. "This is Lumper. What does your dog look like?"

Cookie Breath answered, "Lumper, he's a little yellow puppy. He got lost at a truck stop."

"Uncle Dan . . ." I said softly. I felt scared.

Uncle Dan looked at me, then back at the road. "Easy, Toby," he said. "Let's listen."

More CB calls came over the radio.

"Does he have a black spot on his face?"

"No, he is all yellow."

"Does he have pointy ears?"

"He has long, floppy ears."

"Is he wearing a green ribbon around his neck?"

Cookie Breath said No to all the questions about the lost dog. Then Uncle Dan picked up the CB mike. "Cookie Breath, this is Blue Prince. Which truck stop did you lose your dog at?"

"Tom's Truck Stop," came back the answer.

Then I knew Berf was the missing dog. "But they left him there," I said to Uncle Dan.

"Things are not always as they seem," Uncle Dan said.

"They didn't want him," I said. My eyes were getting wet. And it was hard to swallow again.

"We may not have all the facts."

I remembered Kevin and his grungy clothes.

"Berf loves *us*," I said.

"Toby, how would you feel if it were your dog?"

"Well, 'finders, keepers—losers, weepers,' " I said. But somehow I thought of Ratoid.

"I've heard that saying," Uncle Dan said. "But I like this one better. 'Lost returned is friendship earned.' " He was quiet a minute.

I opened my mouth two or three times. But I couldn't think of what to say.

Finally Uncle Dan said, "What do you think Jesus would do if He found someone's lost dog?"

I was quiet for a few minutes. Then I said, "I think . . . I guess . . . He'd probably . . ."

Uncle Dan handed me the CB mike. "Cookie Breath," I said into the mike. I took a deep breath. "This is Animal Cracker. I have your dog."

Chapter 8

Goodbye to Berf

The kid on the CB yelled, "Dad! Someone found my dog!"

Then a man came on the CB radio. "Animal Cracker, this is Cookie Breath's dad. I'm Bread Dough. Can your driver tell me where you are?"

I handed Uncle Dan the CB mike.

"We're approaching Highway 14, eastbound on Davis Road," he said. "What's your location?"

"We are northbound on 14," said Bread Dough. "About five miles south of Davis."

"There is a rest stop on 14, three-and-a-half miles north of Davis," said Uncle Dan. "We will meet you there." He replaced the mike in its holder. Then he turned the truck toward the ramp to Highway 14.

"What if it's not the same lost dog?" I asked Uncle Dan. I admit I was hoping.

"We'll find out in about twenty minutes," Uncle Dan said.

My thoughts were going wild. What if this kid

was some tough guy? Maybe he was mean to his puppy. And the dog really wanted to get away. Cookie Breath could be part of a gang. Yeah, that's it. And Bread Dough was in on it. They were probably called the Beat-'em-up Bakery Boys.

I pulled Berf onto my lap and put my arms around him. He licked my neck. Well, they weren't going to take my dog. Not without a fight. I was about to warn Uncle Dan when we pulled into the rest stop.

"Can I play with Berf outside? Just for a few minutes?" I asked.

"Sure, Toby," he said. "I think we all need a break."

We all got out of the truck. I played tug of war with Berf and his sock toy. In no time, another eighteen-wheeler pulled into the rest stop. I could see a kid in the cab. And a woman. The kid looked about my age. Maybe a little younger.

Wait a minute. It looked like a girl.

A girl! So much for the gang idea.

Their truck hissed to a stop. The girl was laughing and bouncing up and down. She pointed to Berf. Pretty soon they all got out of their truck.

The girl ran toward Berf. She called, "Ralph! Ralph!" Berf looked around to see her. He barked, "Berf, berf, woof!" and ran toward her.

The man and woman walked toward Uncle Dan and me. They were smiling and waving.

Berf jumped up, and the girl caught him in her arms. "Ralph! I thought you were gone for good," said the girl.

"It looks like your prayers were answered, honey," said the woman.

I wondered about my prayers.

The girl said, "I think so, Mom."

Mom. I remembered my mom's prayer the night before we left. "Help Toby be the best he can be," she had said.

"Oh, Ralph, I missed you so much!" the girl said. He was licking her neck now. I felt my face wet with tears. OK, so sometimes boys cry. Even going-on-third-graders. I guess I was glad for the girl. And for Berf. Or Ralph.

But I sure hated to part with that little yellow dog. Uncle Dan will miss him too, I thought. But he walked toward the other truck driver and the woman.

He said, "I'm Dan Davidson," and put out his hand. "This is my nephew, Toby."

The other driver took his hand and shook it. "I'm Bill Good. My wife Helen and our daughter Jo truck with me for a while every summer." They both shook hands with me and Uncle Dan.

"Toby," said Mr. Good, "you are a fine young man. It must have been hard for you to return Ralph."

Mrs. Good said, "Jo nearly jumped out of the truck when she saw her dog again. We had to move to a new town recently. It has been very hard for her to leave old friends. Your kindness has been a real blessing to her."

"That's OK," I said and looked at Jo and Ralph. I walked to where they were playing.

"Jo—Cookie Breath, I'm Toby—Animal Cracker. Your mom said you have moved to a new town. I did too." I patted Ralph. He wiggled his back end. "A pet sure helps, doesn't it?"

"Yeah," she answered. "Do you have a pet?"

"I did for a little while," I said. "A rat."

"No kidding," she said. "My cousin has a pet rat. I guess they are pretty cool too."

I thought of what the man at Tom's Truck Stop had said. "They said you just left your dog. That you didn't want him anymore. They said people do that sometimes."

"We didn't know he was gone," said Jo. "I was asleep in the bunk. Mom and Dad thought he was too. Until I woke up later and called him."

"Wow," I said. "That must have been awful." I remembered how I felt when I found Ratoid's cage empty.

Just then Mr. Good called, "Jo, it's time to go."

We walked back toward the grown-ups. I said, "Maybe we'll see each other again sometime."

"Maybe so," said Jo.

"Wait a minute," she said suddenly. "I want to give you something." And she ran to their truck. Ralph followed close behind. She climbed in the open door. He climbed right up after her.

Soon she came back out. She had a large paper bag in her hand. Ralph stayed in the truck with Mr. and Mrs. Good. He sat looking out the window.

"This is for you and your uncle," Jo said. She handed me the bag. I looked inside. Cookies! Lots of them! "We have a bakery," Jo said. "Mom runs the baking part. Her CB handle is Muffin Mama. Dad takes care of the shipping." She waved and said goodbye.

Uncle Dan and I climbed back into our truck. Both trucks hissed and started forward. The smell of the cookies made me feel better. Girls aren't so bad, you know. That is, if their mom and dad own a bakery.

Chapter 9

Sharing a Loaf
by the Sea

We delivered the pop bottles on time in Illinois the next day. Uncle Dan was happy about that. He works hard to be known as a good, on-time truck driver. After they unloaded the shipment, Uncle Dan said, "Let's see a few interesting things around here."

"What is there to see?" I asked.

"Well, we're near your old hometown of Chicago, Toby," Uncle Dan said. "When was the last time you got to visit the Museum of Science and Industry? Or saw Lake Michigan?"

"At least a hundred years," I kidded.

"Then I think it's about time to look again. Don't you?"

"Yes!" I shouted. I couldn't help jumping around a little.

Getting the shipping papers all signed and everything didn't take Uncle Dan very long. Then we were bobtailing along the freeway toward Lake Michigan. Bobtailing is driving the truck tractor without a trailer behind it. You have to drive extra safely then, Uncle Dan says. The weight of the trailer helps steady the tractor.

Pretty soon, the endless gray-blue water came into sight. We drove along the road that runs along the western edge of the lake. The water matched the grayness of the cloudy sky. Waves that were taller than I am hit the sandy beach on our right.

Uncle Dan found a place to park the tractor at the museum. The huge building was right across the road from the beach and the lake. "Let's take a walk on the beach first," he said.

"Yeah!" I agreed.

We climbed the steps that led to the crosswalk high above the road. When we got to the top, we stopped and looked around. From up there, we could see for miles and miles. We saw the tall buildings of Chicago to the north. We saw the railways and parks to the south. We saw the museum and the parkways and apartment buildings to the west, behind us. And in front of us was Lake Michigan.

The wind off the lake brought the smell of fish, water, burnt wood—and buttery popcorn.

"Uncle Dan, I'm hungry," I said.

"I see the popcorn stand on the beach is open," Uncle Dan said. "Let's get down there and get some."

I started running toward the downstairs. Uncle Dan laughed and passed me up. But we got down at about the same time. We took off our shoes and tied the laces together. Next, we stuffed our socks inside the shoes and hung them over our shoulders. Then we tramped through the sand toward the little refreshment stand.

"Two buttered popcorns," Uncle Dan said to the vendor. The popcorn man handed each of us a bag heaped high.

"Would you like a cold drink, Toby?"

"Uh-humf," I said with popcorn already in my mouth.

We found an old, water-washed log to sit on. There were not many people on the beach this day. Probably because it was so windy. In fact, the wind kept trying to eat our popcorn. And no one was swimming. There was a sign that read: "NO SWIMMING. DANGEROUS UNDERTOW."

"That means the waves under the water can pull you out into the deep part of the lake really quickly," Uncle Dan said.

Lake Michigan is so big you can't see the other side. I think it must be the size of a small "sea."

"Uncle Dan, do you think Lake Michigan is like the Sea of Galilee?" I asked.

"I don't know, Toby," he answered. "But I can imagine Jesus standing here, teaching great and wonderful things to thousands of people. And you know what else I think of?"

"What?"

"I think of the boy—maybe about your age—who shared his lunch of five little loaves and two fishes. He gave them to Jesus there by the sea. And Jesus worked a miracle and fed all the hungry people with that boy's lunch."

"Wow. I guess even a kid can do something to help people," I said, "especially if the kid lets Jesus do the hard part."

Uncle Dan ruffled up my hair and smiled. "I guess that's about right," he said. When we finished our popcorn, we walked along the beach. I found some great smooth stones and a few shells. I put them in my pocket to take home.

There were also a lot of dead fish on the beach. "The city-park people will clean these up tomorrow," Uncle Dan said. "The high waves have washed them ashore."

"I see a ship out there, Uncle Dan," I said.

"That's a water-processing plant, Toby," he said. "The city of Chicago gets most of its water from Lake Michigan. The pumping building has to be way out there to get the cleaner water."

"Aren't there ships on the lake anymore?"

"Sure. But the harbors are mostly north of here. We'll drive past the yacht harbor after we see the museum. You'll see a lot of boats there."

"Museum!" I remembered. "Can we go now?"

"Let's go," Uncle Dan said.

We brushed the sand off our feet at the steps to the crosswalk. After we put our shoes and socks on, we raced up the stairs. When we got down on the other side, we walked to the museum.

Being in that museum was like being a part of some very important things. We saw the history of cars—with really old cars. We pushed buttons that made wheels turn and things light up. We saw exciting films of finding oil and walked through a model of a human heart. We visited an old-time street with gaslights and everything. We even went through a real World War II submarine and down into a coal mine. I think that was the coolest.

By then I was starving.

"Let's go get something to eat," Uncle Dan said.

"I remember they have a cafeteria here," I said. "It's in the basement."

Uncle Dan and I both picked out a big plate of macaroni and cheese. He got a salad, and I chose broccoli. I like broccoli! And we each got a blue-berry muffin.

But by the time I ate all the macaroni and cheese and the broccoli, I was stuffed. So I decided to save the muffin for a snack in the truck. I wrapped it up in paper napkins for safe-keeping.

We were on our way to the big marble stairs when we saw a bunch of people gathered. They were looking at an old man who lay on the floor. He was kind of moaning and holding his head.

Uncle Dan asked one of the crowd, "What happened?"

"The old guy just fell down the bottom three steps," someone said.

Uncle Dan stooped down next to the man.

"How do you feel, sir?" he asked.

"I just got dizzy. Lost my balance, I guess. Hit my head on the railing."

"Do you feel like sitting up?" Uncle Dan asked.

"I think so," the man said.

People backed away while Uncle Dan helped him to sit up. He sat on the floor next to the old man. "Is anyone here with you?" Uncle Dan asked.

"My grandson is here somewhere," the man said.

"Toby, will you get the gentleman a drink of water?" asked Uncle Dan.

By then, nearly everyone else had walked away. I ran back to the cafeteria and asked for a paper cup. Then I went to the water fountain and filled it.

When I gave it to the man, he looked at me as if I had done something great. Then I remembered the muffin. I had laid it on the step when I went to get the water.

"Here, mister," I said, and handed him the wrapped muffin. "Maybe this will make you feel better."

He smiled and took the muffin and unwrapped it.

"Thank you, son," he said, taking a small bite. "I reckon you have done a good deed for an old man."

Uncle Dan put his hand on the man's shoulder. "Sir, may we say a prayer for you?"

I looked around to see if anyone was watching. It was one thing to pray with the family, I thought. Or at church. I felt funny praying with someone we didn't even know. With strangers watching. I guess I was kind of embarrassed.

Uncle Dan saw me fidgeting. He said very quietly, "Toby, never be ashamed of believing in God. He'll never be ashamed of you."

I guess I needed to be reminded of that. Uncle Dan and I joined hands with the man. We bowed our heads.

"Heavenly Father," Uncle Dan said, "please help this gentleman. Heal any hurts from this fall. Protect him from further injury. We know You love him greatly. We trust You to care for him. Amen."

Just then, a boy a little older than I came running toward us. "Grampa!" he called. "What happened?"

"Why, it's Neil," said the old man. "I guess I forgot where I was for a little bit."

"He fell down a few steps," Uncle Dan said. "He bumped his head, but I think he's OK now. Is there another adult with you?"

"Yes," said the boy. "My mom went out to bring the car to the entrance." The boy hugged his grandfather. The man hugged him back and patted him on the head.

"We were getting ready to leave," the boy said. "Sometimes Grampa forgets stuff. I was staying with him until Mom brought the car around. But we got separated."

"We'll help you get him out to the car," Uncle Dan said. "But be sure to tell your mom what happened. She might want to have a doctor examine him."

Then the old man turned to me and said, "Young man, you have been very kind to a stranger— sharing your little loaf with me. May God bless you always."

I guess I looked kind of funny, standing there with my mouth open. But until then, I never even thought of the muffin as a little loaf. It reminded me of the boy who shared his loaves and fishes with Jesus and with thousands of strangers. It made me feel good all over.

Afterwards, Uncle Dan and I bobtailed to Skokie, north of Chicago. We picked up a trailer load of canned goods to deliver near Rockfield.

On the way home, I thought of all the things we saw and did on this trucking trip. Finding Berf. Losing Berf and making a new friend. Seeing Chicago again—and the lake. Now, it would always remind me of the Sea of Galilee.

But I know I will remember most the old man at the science museum. And that even a kid can do something to help. And it just might turn out to be something big. When Jesus is in charge.

Chapter 10

Surprise, Surprise, Surprise!

The rest of our trip went by fast. We were headed toward Rockfield and home. I kept thinking about Berf and Ratoid. And Kevin. And Mom. As we drove along, Uncle Dan and I sang some songs. He had his harmonica along. He always carries it in his pocket. He says playing it helps him with trucking. He doesn't like the CB on all the time.

Uncle Dan can play almost any song. He really likes to play praise songs. Songs that tell how great God is. I knew some of them from church. So it was fun to sing them together.

And Uncle Dan told some funny stories. About when he was a kid like me. I guess we are a lot alike. Anyway, before long, we pulled into Rockfield. Then we rolled to a stop in front of my house.

Mom came running out the door. I know she heard the air brakes hiss.

"Hi! Hi!" we all hollered. Uncle Dan and I climbed out of the truck. Everyone was hugging everyone else.

"You're just in time for supper," Mom said.

"Do you have a 'truckers special'?" I asked.

She laughed at my joke. "Well, there is plenty of corn bread," she said. "Come and tell me about your trip."

"We can get our things from the truck later," said Uncle Dan.

The sun was low in the sky. The day was almost over. And so was my trucking adventure. At supper we told Mom about the chicken coops. And the Weigh Masters. And talking on the CB. And Berf.

Mom and Uncle Dan looked at each other.

Mom said, "This is not the best time for a puppy, Toby. They cost extra to feed. And you will be in school soon. I have very little time for a puppy right now."

She looked at Uncle Dan again. He cleared his throat—and smiled at her kind of silly.

"I guess God knew the best thing," I said.

And we told her about Chicago. Seeing Lake Michigan and the Museum of Science and Industry again. And the old man. Mom hugged me and told me she was proud of me.

"By the way," Mom said, "Kevin was over today. He asked when you would be home."

"Good," I said. I yawned and stretched. "I'll go see him tomorrow."

Uncle Dan said he would bring our things in. He

was staying overnight.

Mom kidded him, "You just want some trucker flapjacks for breakfast."

He laughed and said, "Yep, that's it."

She turned to me. "Better get to bed, Toby. Tomorrow is another day."

I didn't argue. I was very tired. But I wondered if I could sleep. My head was full of things. I said good night and went upstairs. I didn't have to worry about sleep. I said my prayers and crawled into bed.

Zonk! I was asleep.

I don't even remember turning off the light. But it was off when I woke up. The sun was bright enough. Sun! Today was tomorrow! I jumped out of bed. I heard Mom and Uncle Dan in the kitchen. I washed my face. I combed my hair— sort of. Then I ran downstairs.

"Good morning, sleepyhead," they both said.

Mom put some cherry flapjacks on my plate.

"I'm starving," I said.

"Kevin has been here," Mom said. "He asked if you could come over. I told him you could after breakfast." She poured syrup on my flapjacks. "He seemed to be in an awful hurry about something," she said.

I wondered what it was.

When we finished breakfast, Uncle Dan went to the sink. "Toby, bring your dishes over here," he said. "Let's wash them together. Your mom can start her sewing."

I was fidgety but I said, "Sure." Uncle Dan would be leaving soon. He had that truck load of canned goods to deliver.

Pretty soon we were all standing in the yard. Uncle Dan said to Mom, "Sally, don't work too hard." He said to me, "You are a good trucker, partner." And he ruffled up my hair.

Then he climbed in the truck cab. The engine roared to life. The brakes hissed once more as he pulled away. Then the truck drove out of sight.

I turned to Mom and asked, "Can I go to Kevin's now?"

"How about getting dressed first?" She smiled.

I forgot I still had my pajamas on! I dashed into the house. What could Kevin be in a hurry about? I wondered. I dressed in twenty-six seconds. Almost. Then I was down the stairs. And out the door. I raced through the backyard and climbed the fence. I got the surprise of my life.

There in Kevin's yard was a little yellow dog.

"What?" I said. The dog raced toward me.

"Berf!" I shouted. I picked him up. He began licking my neck. Kevin came out of his house. A girl followed close behind.

Jo! What was she doing here?

Kevin was laughing. "Toby! This is my cousin Jo Good!"

I couldn't believe it. Kevin kept talking. "Aunt Helen and Uncle Bill picked me up at my grandma's. I rode home in their truck. This is Ralph."

"I know," I said. "We've met."

We all laughed happily. Each of us told our part of the story to the others. Over and over. We were all excited.

Then Kevin said, "Come in, Toby. I want to show you something."

"There's more?" I asked. He laughed and shoved me in front of him. Jo opened the door.

"Wait here," Kevin said in the kitchen. He went into another room. In a few minutes, he came back with something in a shoe box. It had holes punched on top. He put the box on the table. And slowly raised the lid.

I could not believe my eyes!

A rat! A black-and-white rat!

I looked closer. "Is that . . . ?"

"Yup. It's Ratoid," Kevin said. He had a big grin on his face.

"I don't get it," I said.

Jo said, "Remember, I told you my cousin had a rat." She patted the rat. "Well, it was one he found." Jo was as excited as I was.

"How?" I asked. I was still in shock.

"Your mom said he got out your window," Kevin said. "So after you left, I thought I'd take a look around. You know that tree outside your window? I found him inside the tire swing." He sounded like a TV detective.

"I figure he climbed along the branch. Then down the rope. Rats can do that."

"Wow," I said.

"So now you've got Ratoid back," Kevin said.

"You mean, you're giving him back to me?" I said. "You could have kept him. I wouldn't even have known."

"You are my friend," Kevin said.

Suddenly I remembered Uncle Dan's saying. "Lost returned is friendship earned." I guess he really was right.

We took turns petting Ratoid. Then I put him back in the box.

"Jo has to leave now," Kevin said. "But she will be back tomorrow."

"Yeah," Jo said. "I live in Rockfield now."

"Is this the new town you moved to?" I could believe anything now.

"Yes," she answered. "We moved our bakery here. My Aunt Lorry, Kevin's mom, will be able to work there. So you will be seeing Ralph a lot."

I had to sit down. How could so many things happen? I thought. In just one week!

Mom once said, "Trusting God is the greatest adventure there is." Boy, was she ever right. As I was about to see in the next few days.

Chapter 11

A Treehouse Disaster

The Goods went to settle their new home here in Rockfield. They left Ralph with Kevin and his mom. After Jo left, Kevin and I played with the dog and the rat for a while. We made a kind of tunnel out of some big cardboard boxes.

But, no matter what, Ralph wouldn't run through it. And Ratoid just wouldn't "fetch" the little ball we tossed around.

Two easy things, we thought. After all, Ratoid could run through a tunnel with no problem. And Ralph would catch any old ball. But I guess dogs will be dogs, and rats will be rats.

So we started putting a fort together from the same cardboard boxes. Then Kevin said, "Hey, a tree fort would be great!" He found a piece of rope and climbed the tree outside my bedroom window. I tied the boxes to the end of the rope he let down. He pulled them up and asked me to climb up.

"Bring a hammer and some nails," he ordered.

"Kevin, those boxes aren't very strong," I said.

"They're strong enough," he said.

He began to stack them on two branches. I went into the garage and found the toolbox.

"Mom, Kevin and I need the hammer and some nails," I called.

"Be sure to put the hammer back," she answered from the kitchen.

I put them in a pail and carried them out to the tree. Kevin lowered the rope, and I tied it to the pail handle. After he hauled it up, I climbed up to join him.

"Nail that box right there," Kevin said. "That will be the main part of the fort."

"Kevin," I said again, "I don't think these boxes are very strong. They might not hold us."

"I've seen other tree forts made of boxes," he answered. "Lots of people do it."

I like Kevin, but sometimes he's stubborn. I didn't want to argue with him. So I nailed the larger of the boxes to where two branches joined. I must have pounded twenty nails in that thing. I think I just kept hammering nails in the box just so it wouldn't get finished.

Finally, Kevin said, "That's good enough, give me the hammer. I'll nail this box above for a tower."

I sat on a branch and handed nails to Kevin. He pounded away on the "tower" box. I didn't say much, but I kept thinking, This will never work. I know it's not the right way to build a treehouse.

Then, Kevin handed me the hammer. "OK, that should do it for the tower," he said. "Toby, you get into the main part and try it out."

"Me?"

"Sure. Somebody's got to test it. And it's your tree."

That made some sense. But not enough. I said, "How about Ralph? He's a pretty smart dog. I think he should have the honor. Unless you want to do it. As the leader, I mean."

Kevin paid no attention to the honor I had just given him.

"OK, get the dog," he said. After a lot of commanding, coaxing, barking, and shoving, Ralph was up the tree. I thought of using the rope to haul him up once. But I figured one of us was sure to get hung.

Finally, Kevin and I lifted Ralph into the main part of the fort. Ralph turned around two or three times and laid down.

"See?" Kevin said. "No problem." He shook the box Ralph lay in to prove his point.

Shaking the box scared Ralph, I guess. The next thing we knew, Ralph was scrambling over the edge of the box.

"Grab him!" Kevin yelled.

I made a lunge and caught a dog leg as Ralph

went over the side. When I tried to balance myself, my foot went into the box. Actually, it went through the bottom of the box.

"Hold him! Hold him!" shouted Kevin as my chin hit the edge of the box.

Kevin slid down the tree and reached his arms up toward Ralph and me.

"OK, let him go," he hollered.

I had no choice, anyway. Ralph twisted loose and fell toward Kevin. Kevin caught him. Sort of. They both landed in a heap on the ground.

I don't know which one of them yelped louder. Ralph ran under some bushes. Kevin sat rubbing a bump on his head. And I worked my leg loose from the hole in the box and climbed down the tree. I sat next to Kevin, rubbing my scraped chin.

Just then, Mom called, "Supper!"

"Gotta go," I said to Kevin.

"That's OK. I better go too. I'll see you tomorrow. Don't forget, Jo will be here."

"Right. See you," I said.

I picked up the hammer and headed for the garage. I thought to myself, From now on, I'm going to be tougher. When I think something is not right, I'm going to stick by it.

During spaghetti, Mom told me about some strange tropical fish she saw at a customer's house. I think she was trying to hint about what kind of pet *she* would like.

During chocolate cake, I told her about the tree fort. And Kevin's way of making me feel I should do things his way.

"I knew all along it wasn't the right way," I said. "But Kevin sort of made me feel dumb not to do what he said. Sort of like I'd better do it his way if I wanted to stay friends. He didn't exactly say that. But that's the way I felt."

"That feeling is what they call 'peer pressure,' Toby," Mom said. She explained more. "Peer pressure is when friends your own age speak or dress or act in a certain way. Then if you speak or dress or act in a way that's different from theirs, you feel left out. Like you're not a part of the group.

"That's a lot of pressure for a kid, I know. But it happens. Friends of yours may try to get you to do things that you know are wrong. They may even make fun of you or leave you out if you don't do them."

"Well, I think that's crummy," I said. "But what can I do about it?"

Mom was quiet a minute. Then she asked, "Toby, do you remember the Bible story about Daniel?"

"Sure. He was thrown into a lions' den."

"Yes, he was. And some of his friends were thrown into a blazing furnace. Do you know why?"

"Well, they didn't obey the king."

"Yes, but it was more than that," Mom said.

"Those smart young men—Daniel, Shadrach, Meshach, and Abednego—refused to go along with what everyone else was doing. They were living in Babylon, but they were Israelites. King Nebuchadnezzar knew how smart they were. So he was training them to work for him."

Mom went on. "He wanted the four young men to eat certain foods they knew were bad for them. And to worship some statues the king said were gods. Everyone was doing it. But Daniel, Shadrach, Meshach, and Abednego said they would not do what everyone else was doing. Even if the king said so," Mom said.

"Even if he killed them," she added. "They said they would only obey their God—our God."

"Wow. That was brave!"

"Daniel, Shadrach, Meshach, and Abednego were all saved by God. But it sometimes takes a lot of courage to resist peer pressure—or 'king pressure,' " Mom said with a smile.

I would remember that in a few short days. But now it was time to help Mom with the dishes and get my bath.

In my bed that night, I thought of Kevin and the tree fort. I thought of Daniel and his three friends from the Bible. And I thought of Jo and Ralph.

I was dreaming of being in a pit with a lion— only the lion looked more like Ralph. He was roaring, but it sounded more like, "Berf!"

Kevin was in the dream too. He was dressed in robes and some kind of cardboard crown. He kept saying, "Better eat that rope. Everybody does it."

Then Mom called, "Breakfast!" and I woke up.

Chapter 12

A Dead Bird and a Road Sign

While I was polishing off my second helping of eggs, Mom was acting pretty strange. Finally, she said, "Toby, I got a call from Lorry this morning."

"Kevin's mom?"

"Yes. She said Jo and her mother are going to stay with her a few days. And Kevin is going trucking to Evansville with his Uncle Bill."

I thought, Oh, boy. Here I am with just a girl to play with. For days. I mean, she wasn't just any old girl. But she wasn't a guy, either. Boring. Boring. Boring.

Then Mom said, "Bill has invited you to go along with him and Kevin. Would you like to do that?"

Would a rat like a hunk of cheese?

"Yes!" I said, grabbing a piece of air with my fist. Then I added more calmly, "I mean, yes, I definitely would like to go."

I stood up and headed for the door. "When do we leave?"

81

"Just hold on," laughed Mom. "Maybe you'd like to pack a few things?"

"Oh," I said. "Right."

I turned to go upstairs.

"I'll fix some snacks for you to take along," Mom said. In a half-hour, Kevin and I were climbing up into the truck's tractor cab. Jo's dad Bill was sitting behind the steering wheel. And Ralph was in the bunk. The engine was running loudly.

"Ralph is one of the guys too," Bill said. Kevin and I grinned at each other. He crawled in the bunk with Ralph. I sat on the seat next to the driver's seat.

Mom stepped up on the lowest step. She had the box of snacks in her hand. "Come, give me a hug," she called. We traded snacks for hugs. Kevin's mom did the same.

Jo just yelled, "Hurry back, guys!" And we began to rumble down the street.

We didn't say much while we drove through town. We were too busy watching the buildings slide by. They sure looked different from the truck. After a while, Bill turned on the CB radio. He said, "Let's see what's happening out there."

It was always fun to hear the different "handles," or radio names. We had to laugh at some of them: "Two-beans," "Turtle," "Ice Cream," and "Lunch Man."

Seemed a lot of them were about food. Which reminded Kevin and me of our snacks. We mostly munched and read and wrestled with Ralph that first day. And stopped for food and gas, of course.

Kevin and Ralph and I slept in the bunk that night at a rest stop. Bill made a kind of bunk out of the front seats for himself.

The truck was rolling again before the sun came up. Kevin and I were counting horses in the passing fields, when Bill said, "Hold on tight, boys!"

We saw a whole bunch of cars and trucks in the road ahead. Bill slowed the truck down with a lot of quick gear shifting. The air brakes went "*Psss-s-s-s, tssss-s-s-s-s!*" We held tight to our seats during the jerky ride. Finally, we pulled to a stop on the gravelly shoulder of the road.

"You boys stay put while I see what's going on," said Bill. He climbed down out of the truck cab. He left the door open and the engine running. Kevin climbed into the driver's seat. He began sliding his hands around on the steering wheel.

"You better be careful, Kev," I said.

"What could happen?" Kevin said, pretending to shift. "*Brrrr-rr-r-r-mmmm*," he said, copying the sound of the engine.

He was making me nervous. "I wonder what happened," I said, trying to get him to think of something else.

"Let's go find out," Kevin said.

He clipped Ralph's leash on him and started climbing down from the truck with the dog.

"Kevin?" I called.

"C'mon!" he answered.

I'd better stay with him, I thought, and climbed out after him and Ralph. I ran behind them toward the cluster of cars and trucks ahead. People were wandering all around. As we got closer, we saw police cars—three of them. Two were empty. In the third one, a police officer was talking on his radio. I wondered about Bill.

"Do you see your uncle anywhere?" I asked Kevin. He didn't answer—he just walked over to a police officer who was writing something in a notebook.

"What happened, officer?" Kevin asked.

Leave it to ol' Kev to get to the bottom of things in a hurry.

The police officer didn't look up from his notebook. "Goat," he said.

"Goat?" Kevin and I repeated together and looked at each other.

"Goat in the road. Car swerved to miss him. The rest were following too closely on damp pavement. One truck jackknifed. Blocked the road from both directions."

The police officer closed his notebook and put the pen in his pocket. "Take a month of Sundays to untangle this mess," he said. Then he seemed to notice us for the first time. He looked at us over his sunglasses and said, "Bunch of dented vehicles. Nobody hurt much. Where do you boys belong?"

"My uncle's probably helping up there," Kevin said. And he nodded toward the mess of vehicles.

"You boys and your dog better get back with your vehicle," said the officer.

"Right," I said, grabbing Kevin's sleeve. We were headed toward our truck when Ralph jerked loose from Kevin.

"Oh, great," I moaned. And we both took off after him.

"Ralph! Ralph!" we shouted.

"Here, boy! Stay! Sit! Down! Ralph, stop!"

He wove in and out between people and cars, and we followed. Finally, Ralph spied something on the ground. A dead bird.

He grabbed it between his teeth, almost grinning, and trotted back to us. I latched on to his leash and called to Kevin, "I've got him! Come on!"

At last, we headed back to the truck. On the way, Kevin spotted a road sign lying on the ground: SLOW—CURVES AHEAD. The sign must have been knocked off its post by one of the vehicles in the pileup.

Kevin picked up the sign and kept walking toward our truck.

"Hey, Kevin," I said. "You planning to keep that sign?"

"Sure, Toby. It'll look cool in our tree fort."

"We don't have a tree fort," I reminded him. "And the sign should be put back. It's a warning to drivers."

"Don't be a baby," Kevin said. "Everybody does it."

I suddenly thought of Daniel—and Shadrach, Meshach, and Abednego. "Not everybody, Kev. It's wrong. And it could cause an accident. Shadrach wouldn't do it."

"Huh?"

"Or Meshach, either."

"Who?"

"And I seriously doubt if Abednego would keep the sign."

"Toby, I do believe you have slipped out of gear. What are you talking about?"

By then we were back at the truck. I thought to myself, Here I am with a dog with a dead bird in his mouth—which he is not about to give up. And a pal with a stolen road sign—which *he* is not about to give up.

Bill was still nowhere in sight. So I decided it was up to me. "OK, Kevin. Let's sit here outside the truck. I'll tell you about those guys." I turned to Ralph and ordered, "Sit!" Which, to my surprise, he did.

Kevin leaned the sign against the big truck tire, and we sat next to Ralph. "Ever heard of Daniel, the Bible guy?" I asked Kevin.

"The one who was thrown in a lions' den?" he said.

"Yeah. Well, have you ever heard about his three friends?"

"I figure you're gonna tell me," said Kevin, with a grin.

Ralph lay down with the bird between his front paws.

I began the story of Daniel and King Nebuchadnezzar—and Shadrach, Meshach, and Abednego.

I guess I described the fierce, hungry lions and the roaring, hot flames of the furnace pretty well. Kevin was really listening. And I think I got the part over about not doing what everybody else does—peer pressure—pretty well too. And the courage it takes sometimes to stand up for what you know is right.

Anyway, just about then, Bill came walking toward us with another man. Ralph forgot his bird and jumped up, tail wagging, to greet Bill.

"You boys OK?" Bill asked.

"Fine," we answered, standing.

"This is Sam," he said. "He drives a truck, too, and needs a ride to a phone. His rig is jammed in the middle of that mess."

We said Hi, grabbed Ralph and climbed up into the bunk of the truck. Kevin called over his shoulder, "Oh, Uncle Bill, that sign by the tire goes back by that post over there."

As Bill took the sign back, Kevin said, "Know any more of those Bible stories?"

"Sure," I said. "We hear some great ones at my church every week." Bill and Sam climbed into the truck, and one of the police officers signaled us where to turn around.

As we headed back the way we came, Kevin said, "So. Maybe I could come to your church sometime."

Chapter 13

The Biggest Adventure of All

We got home from our trucking trip on Tuesday. Kevin and I were pretty well wiped out.

So was Ralph, I think. He kept forgetting to bark. He would start out with a "Buh . . . buh . . ." Then after a few minutes he would end up with the ". . . Erf!"

Bill and Helen were almost finished getting their new house in order. On Wednesday morning, Kevin and Jo and I helped put a few more things in their places. Then we went out to check the tree fort. Or what was supposed to be a tree fort. All that was left was some wet cardboard hanging down from the branches. And the "tower" box Kevin had nailed above it for a roof.

"What we need is some real wood boards," Kevin said. "Those cardboard boxes just won't hold up."

No kidding, I thought to myself.

"Especially if it rains or something," Kevin went on.

Or someone puts their foot through the "floor," I thought.

"I think Dad has some old boards," Jo said. "Let's go ask." We rode our bikes to the Goods' house and found Bill at home. He was stacking some packing boxes in the garage.

"Dad!" called Jo. "We need some boards. Are there any here that we could have?"

"What do you need them for?" Bill asked.

"Our tree fort," Kevin said. "We need a strong floor."

"How about a piece of plywood?" Bill asked. We followed him behind the garage. He pulled a big square piece of wood out of a stack.

"Perfect!" we all agreed.

"How will you brace it?" Bill asked.

"The branches we're building it on are in a 'V' shape," I answered.

"That should do it," he said. "Be sure to use plenty of strong nails."

"We will," Kevin said.

We balanced the plywood on Jo's bike and walked it back to my house.

Getting the plywood up in the tree was not easy. We finally pounded a couple of big nails in it for "hooks." Then Kevin climbed up to the branches we would use for the support. Jo and I tied one end of the rope around the nails. We threw the other end to Kevin. He looped it over a higher branch and swung to the ground on it.

All three of us pulled on the rope, and the plywood began to move upward. It finally passed the V-branches.

"Hold it right there!" ordered Kevin.

Jo and I tugged at the rope, trying to hold it steady. Kevin climbed back up the tree and guided the plywood into place.

At last he stood on it and declared it perfect. Then we sent the pail with hammer and nails in it up on the rope. I climbed up to help with the nailing. After a while, Kevin climbed down and gave Jo a turn at hammering.

We nailed some of the heavier cardboard around three sides for "walls." The old "tower" box still made a good roof. About 2,458 nails later, we decided it was a finished tree fort. And we hauled up three old chair cushions mom gave us . Finally, we held our first club meeting.

Kevin was pretty boastful about building the fort. "Yep, if you want something built right, just ask ol' Kev."

"Seems to me you had a little help," Jo said.

"And how about the floor you're sitting on, ol' Kev?" I chimed in.

"Yeah, I'd like to have seen you even get that up in the tree without us," Jo said.

"I guess it was a pretty big building job for one person," Kevin admitted.

"Makes me think of Noah building the ark," I said. I don't know why I said it.

"Noah!" said Kevin and Jo.

"Well, yeah," I defended myself. "Noah and his family built this huge kind of a houseboat—about the size of a football field, I think. And three stories high. Then they had to cover it with this sticky stuff to make it waterproof."

"I know about the animals," Kevin said. "Two-by-two he loaded them on the boat."

"Well-l-l-l," I said, "actually, the animals weren't all loaded in two-by-two."

"What were they, then, two-by-fours?" Kevin laughed at his little joke.

Jo asked, "How were they loaded, Toby?"

"*Seven* of each of the animals that God called clean were put on the ark. Just the ones God called unclean were loaded in twos."

I looked at Kevin and Jo. Their faces clearly said, "Right, wise guy!"

"Really!" I said. "I learned it in my church-school class. There are a lot of neat adventures in the Bible."

Still they were quiet. "Really!" I said again.

Finally, Kevin asked, "OK, are there any other boat adventures?"

"Sure," I answered. "Like when the apostle Paul went on this ship, and there was a storm. And the ship fell apart, but nobody died—because Paul was on the ship, and God was protecting him. Then he was bitten by a poisonous snake on an island but didn't die. And the natives wanted to make him one of their gods, and . . ."

Kevin interrupted. "You learned all of that stuff at your church?" he asked.

"Sure."

"And being a Christian is really an adventure?"

"Mom says trusting God is the biggest adventure there is."

"What do *you* say?"

Suddenly I felt like I was in a very warm spotlight. Then I remembered what Uncle Dan had said: "Never be ashamed of believing in God, Toby. He will never be ashamed of you."

I looked at Kevin and swallowed. Then I smiled.

"I say so too."

Then I went on, "Jesus has been my Friend for a long, long time. I trust Him because I never doubt that He loves me. And we have a lot of adventures together."

Kevin got quiet. I can always tell when he's really thinking. He gets this kind of faraway look and rubs his hand through his hair real slowly. At last he slapped his knee and said, "Then I'll do it!"

"Do it?"

"I'll trust God."

"Tell *Him*, Kevin. Not me," I said.

Until then, Jo had been pretty quiet. But now she said softly, "Me too."

"Jo?" I looked at her.

"Me too, I'll trust God to be my Friend."

Just as Jo and Kevin finished asking God to be their Friend forever, we heard Mom calling, "Toby!"

"We're in the fort, Mom!" I answered.

"Well, come on down," she said from below us. "Your Aunt Zazu is stopping by."

Aunt Zazu is Mom's sister. She trains birds for a show she runs. Kevin, Jo, and I leaned over the cardboard walls of our tree fort.

"Does she have any of her show birds with her?" I asked.

"No," answered Mom. "She's on her way to the lake. She has to get her houseboat ready to sail. The birds are already on board."

"A boat?" Kevin said, with a gleam in his eye.

"Show birds?" Jo said.

"Do you know where I might find three kids who would like to help?" asked Mom.

The three of us looked at each other. And slid down the tree.

A FAITH-BUILDING

ADVENTURE

DETECTIVE
ZACK
and the Secrets in the Sand
by Jerry Thomas

Detective Zack is back!

This time Zack and his dad head for the Middle East and more mystery. Between escaping deadly snakes and riding knobby-kneed camels, Zack and his new friend Achmed uncover secrets in the sand about heroes and famous places from the Old Testament.

But even as evidence to support the Bible stories grows, so do the questions. Did fire really fall down from heaven and destroy Sodom? And what about the man with the red hat?

US$7.95/
Cdn$10.75.
Paper.

**Look for
Detective Zack
at your local
Christian
bookstore.**

© 1992 Pacific
Press Publishing
Association
479/9751b